TEN *Thank-You* LETTERS

DANIEL KIRK

Nancy Paulsen Books ✺ An Imprint of Penguin Group (USA)

for Aiden

NANCY PAULSEN BOOKS
Published by the Penguin Group
Penguin Group (USA) LLC
375 Hudson Street
New York, NY 10014

USA | Canada | UK | Ireland | Australia
New Zealand | India | South Africa | China
penguin.com
A Penguin Random House Company

Copyright © 2014 by Daniel Kirk.
Penguin supports copyright. Copyright fuels creativity, encourages diverse voices,
promotes free speech, and creates a vibrant culture. Thank you for buying an authorized
edition of this book and for complying with copyright laws by not reproducing, scanning,
or distributing any part of it in any form without permission. You are supporting writers
and allowing Penguin to continue to publish books for every reader.

Library of Congress Cataloging-in-Publication Data
Kirk, Daniel. Ten thank-you letters / Daniel Kirk. pages cm
Summary: While Pig is trying to finish a thank-you note to his grandmother,
his best friend Rabbit repeatedly interrupts to borrow supplies for a series
of his own notes, thanking all of the special people in their lives.
[1. Thank-you notes—Fiction. 2. Gratitude—Fiction. 3. Best friends—Fiction.
4. Friendship—Fiction.] I. Title.
PZ7.K6339Tek 2014 [E]—dc23 2013046403

Manufactured in China.
ISBN 978-0-399-16937-3
Special Markets ISBN 978-0-399-17691-3 Not for Resale
3 5 7 9 10 8 6 4

Design by Annie Ericsson. Title hand lettering by Annie Ericsson.
Text set in Century Schoolbook Penguin Infant and Tyke ITC Std.
The illustrations in this book were made by scanning ink-on-paper drawings and
painted plywood panels into the computer and adding textures and colors in Photoshop.

This Imagination Library edition is published by Penguin Young Readers, a division
of Penguin Random House, exclusively for Dolly Parton's Imagination Library,
a not-for-profit program designed to inspire a love of reading and learning, sponsored
in part by The Dollywood Foundation. Penguin's trade editions of this work are
available wherever books are sold.

Hello, Rabbit.

Hello, Pig.
Want to play?

Okay, Pig, I am done
with my letter.
How about you?

Not yet, Rabbit, I am
telling my grandma
about the weather.

But it's a thank-you letter! Why tell her about the weather?

I don't know, Rabbit, it's just the way I do it.

Whoa, I just thought of someone who deserves a BIG thank-you! Can I borrow another piece of paper, Pig?

And an envelope, and a stamp, too?

Chores?
Why are you
telling her that?
It's a thank-you
letter!

Because Grandma likes it
when I help my mom,
and she might want to
know how things are
going around here.

Hey, I just thought of another
great person to thank.
Can I borrow more paper?

Dear Mr. Lapin,
In case you were wondering how things are going around here, they are great!
Your funny books make my whole class laugh.
Love,
Rabbit

Aren't you done with your letter yet, Pig?

No, Rabbit.
I just want to tell
Grandma that
I laughed so much
yesterday my loose
tooth came out!

Can I have another sheet of paper, Pig?
Let me guess, you thought of someone else to thank?
I sure did!

This one's done, too. How is your letter going, Pig?

Well, I haven't seen my grandma in a while, so there's a lot to tell her. But you keep interrupting!

Sorry, Pig! Maybe if you just
give me a stack of paper
and envelopes and more stamps,
I won't have to bother you!

Dear Mr. Kidd,
Thanks for delivering all our mail. It's a lot to carry, isn't it?
Love,
Rabbit

There, I am finished!
See you later, Pig.
I am off to the mailbox
to send my letters!

Finally, I can finish
my letter . . . Yay, done!

But . . . Rabbit
used all my
envelopes!
And all of the
stamps!

Ring!
Ring!

Hello, Pig.
Guess what?
I got more
envelopes
and stamps
for you.

And I wrote one more
thank-you letter.
I thought I'd deliver
it myself. Here!

Thanks, Rabbit!
No one ever wrote me
a thank-you letter before!

Dear Pig,
Thank you for
inspiring me.
And for being
generous. And
for being my friend!
Love,
Rabbit
P.S. Now are you ready
to play catch?

Yay! Game time!

Yes—after a quick stop at the mailbox!